Short Inspiring Sport Stories For Kids

Spectacular Stories For Young Readers Ages 7-11

Mahdi Amini

Introduction

Welcome, dear readers! If you're seeking a thrilling escape into the world of stories for kids and adults or if you're in the market for beautifully designed notebooks, I invite you to visit my author page. It's your gateway to a realm of chilling narratives and exquisite stationery.

Thank you "Mahdi Amini"

Please rate my book if you like it

The Little Goalkeeper's Dream

In the heart of Sunnyville, where the sun seemed to shine a bit brighter, lived a spirited young boy named Jake. From the tender age of three, soccer had become Jake's world. His backyard echoed with the constant thud of the ball against his small, determined feet.

As Jake grew older, so did his dreams. He idolized the legendary goalkeepers he watched on television, imagining himself making miraculous saves in front of cheering crowds. His ambition was infectious, and soon, the neighborhood kids joined him in impromptu soccer matches, with Jake guarding the goal like a miniature superhero.

One day, a colorful poster caught Jake's eye—an announcement for the annual Sunnyville Soccer Tournament. Eager to prove himself, Jake rallied his friends, and together they formed the Sunnyville Strikers. Training sessions became a daily ritual, each one more intense than the last. Jake's father, a former soccer player himself, became his coach, imparting invaluable wisdom about resilience and teamwork.

The tournament day arrived with a burst of energy and excitement. The Strikers, led by their fearless goalkeeper, took the field with determination written all over their faces. The matches were fierce, but Jake's acrobatic saves and unwavering spirit caught the attention of everyone present.

In a crucial moment, during a penalty shootout, the opposing team stood ready. Jake focused, visualizing success. As the ball zoomed towards the goal, he leaped like a soaring eagle, deflecting the shot with a jaw-dropping save. The crowd erupted into applause, and a wave of pride washed over Jake.

The news of Jake's incredible feat spread like wildfire. Representatives from the renowned Sunnyville Soccer Academy, impressed by his natural talent, approached Jake's family with an offer. They believed he had the potential to become a soccer legend.

Despite the excitement, challenges awaited Jake at the academy. Rigorous training sessions, competitive matches, and homesickness tested his resilience. But with every setback, Jake learned to bounce back stronger, fueled by his unwavering dream.

As seasons passed, Jake's prowess as a goalkeeper became legendary. His story inspired a new generation of soccer enthusiasts in Sunnyville and beyond. The once-little boy with a big dream had become a symbol of determination, proving that with passion, hard work, and a dash of courage, anyone could achieve their goals.

"The Little Goalkeeper's Dream" wasn't just a story in Sunnyville; it became a saga of triumph, resilience, and the unyielding pursuit of one's dreams, reminding every child that the sky is not the limit; it's just the beginning of their own remarkable journey.

The Star Striker's Ascent

In the bustling town of Victoryville, where soccer was more than just a sport, lived a spirited young girl named Mia. From her very first kick, Mia's love for the game was evident. Her nimble footwork and goal-scoring prowess set her apart, earning her the nickname "Mia Magic."

As Mia grew older, her aspirations soared higher. She dreamt of becoming a forward, dazzling the world with her skillful maneuvers and scoring goals that echoed in the hearts of fans. Mia's bedroom walls were adorned with posters of legendary forwards, each one a beacon lighting her path to greatness.

Undeterred by the doubters who thought soccer was a boys' game, Mia practiced tirelessly. She joined the local youth team, where her lightning-quick sprints and precise shots left spectators in awe. Mia's father, her biggest cheerleader, constructed a makeshift goal in their backyard, and under the starry night sky, Mia perfected her signature moves.

One day, news of a national youth soccer tournament reached Victoryville. Mia, fueled by determination, tried out for the team, earning her spot as the youngest forward. The tournament became Mia's proving ground, and with every goal she scored, her confidence soared.

As fate would have it, a talent scout from the renowned Stellar Strikers Academy witnessed Mia's brilliance on the field. The academy, known for shaping soccer prodigies, extended an invitation to Mia. Overwhelmed with excitement, she packed her bags, ready for the journey that awaited her.

Life at Stellar Strikers was challenging, but Mia's passion fueled her resilience. Guided by experienced coaches, she honed her skills, each training session bringing her closer to her dream of becoming the best forward in the world. Mia's journey was not without setbacks, but with every stumble, she rose stronger, learning the art of perseverance.

Years passed, and Mia emerged as a star striker, dazzling the soccer world with her artistry on the field. Her name echoed in stadiums globally, and Victoryville beamed with pride. Mia's story wasn't just about soccer; it was a testament to the power of dreams, breaking stereotypes, and proving that true magic lies within the heart of those who dare to dream big.

"The Star Striker's Ascent" became more than a story in Victoryville; it became a anthem of inspiration for every child with a soccer ball and a dream, reminding them that the journey to greatness begins with a single kick.

Sprinting to Stardom

In the vibrant town of Marathon Meadows, a young girl named Alex had a passion that set her apart—track and field. From a tender age, Alex's nimble feet raced against the wind, leaving a trail of determination in her wake. Her heart belonged to the track, and the rhythmic sound of spikes against the asphalt became her anthem.

As Alex grew, so did her dreams. She aspired to become the fastest athlete in the world, her eyes set on the grand stage of international competitions. Her room adorned with posters of legendary sprinters, Alex drew inspiration from their achievements, promising herself she'd leave her mark on the tracks of history.

Undeterred by skeptics who believed track and field was reserved for the swiftest, Alex trained tirelessly. The local track became her second home, where she sprinted under the watchful gaze of the setting sun. Her parents, her biggest supporters, cheered her on from the stands, their voices echoing like a melody of encouragement.

News of the National Youth Sprinting Championship reached Marathon Meadows, and Alex seized the opportunity. The track felt like a runway to her dreams, and with every stride, she sprinted closer to her aspirations. The gold medal hanging from her neck was not just a symbol of victory but a ticket to the world stage.

A prestigious sports academy recognized Alex's talent, offering her a scholarship to hone her skills. Guided by experienced coaches, Alex transformed into a force of nature on the track. The hurdles she faced only fueled her determination, and the finish line became a gateway to endless possibilities.

As the years unfolded, Alex emerged as one of the world's best athletes, her name echoing in stadiums across the globe. Marathon Meadows, once a quaint town, now beamed with pride, and young athletes looked to Alex as a beacon of inspiration. Her story wasn't just about running; it was a narrative of resilience, unwavering belief, and the triumph of a young girl sprinting her way to stardom.

"Sprinting to Stardom" became a tale etched in Marathon Meadows' history, inspiring generations to come. The track wasn't just a field of competition for Alex; it was a canvas where she painted her dreams with every step, proving that with perseverance, even the smallest towns could produce the fastest athletes.

Skyward Shooter

In the bustling city of Hoopington, there lived a
young boy named Jake whose heart beat to the
rhythm of bouncing basketballs. His hands gripped
the ball with a passion that foretold greatness, and
his eyes saw the hoop as a gateway to the stars.
Jake's dream wasn't just to play basketball; it was
to become the best rebounder and three-point
shooter the world had ever seen.

From the neighborhood courts to the polished
floors of the school gym, Jake's journey began. His
lanky frame defied expectations as he soared to
grasp rebounds that seemed destined for others.
The basketball court became his proving ground,
and with every missed shot, Jake saw an
opportunity to rise.

Dusk till dawn, Jake practiced his three-pointers,
the echo of swishes and misses harmonizing with
his dreams. His backyard hoop became a portal to a
future where the net would tremble at the accuracy
of his shots. Jake's parents, watching from the
porch, believed in their son's celestial aspirations.

The pivotal moment arrived during the city's Junior
Basketball League. Jake's team faced formidable
opponents, but he stood tall, both in stature and
spirit. Rebounding like a human spring and
shooting three-pointers with celestial precision,

Jake led his team to victory. The crowd erupted, and Jake's name echoed through the arena like a victorious anthem.

Colleges scouted Jake, recognizing his unique talent. He joined the prestigious Skyward Academy, where the court stretched beneath an open sky. Coaches refined his skills, and teammates marveled at the boy whose rebounds seemed to defy gravity and whose three-pointers painted the sky with success.

As Jake soared through professional leagues, his reputation as the "Skyward Shooter" spread like wildfire. Opponents feared his rebounds, and the crowd held its breath as he aimed for the three-point line. Awards adorned Jake's shelves, but the gleam in his eyes told a story beyond accolades—a story of a boy who turned his love for basketball into a journey reaching the celestial heights of his dreams.

"Skyward Shooter" became a legend in Hoopington, a story shared among aspiring athletes. Jake's journey wasn't just about conquering rebounds and three-pointers; it was a testament to the belief that with determination and a love for the game, one could shoot for the stars and touch them.

Gridiron Glory

In the small town of Triumphville, where dreams lingered like the scent of freshly cut grass, lived a boy named Tim. Tim wasn't the fastest, strongest, or biggest, but his heart cradled a passion for American football that surpassed any physical limitation. Triumphville High School's football field became Tim's sanctuary, and the cheers of the crowd, his inspiration.

Tim's journey began as the water boy, an observer of gridiron glory from the sidelines. His slender frame often made him an easy target for bullies, but within him, a fire ignited with each touchdown and echoing cheer. The football players, noticing Tim's unwavering spirit, invited him to join their practices, transforming him from the water boy to the heartbeat of the team.

Triumphville High faced formidable opponents, but Tim's determination became the catalyst for triumph. Despite his size, he darted through defenses like a wisp of wind, earning him the nickname "Swift Sparrow." His connection with the quarterback was so seamless that it seemed like they shared a telepathic link on the field.

As the seasons unfolded, so did Tim's prowess. He transformed from the quiet boy on the sidelines to the indomitable force on the gridiron. Triumphville

High clinched championships, and Tim's underdog story became the heartbeat of the town. His journey inspired a generation, teaching them that strength wasn't just in muscles but in resilience and a love for the game.

Colleges scouted Tim, and he earned a scholarship to the prestigious Gridiron University. Tim faced opponents twice his size, but his agility, determination, and the lessons from Triumphville turned him into a formidable force. The Swift Sparrow soared through the college leagues, leaving a trail of victories in his wake.

Tim's story reached the professional leagues, where he donned the jersey of the Triumph Falcons. The cheers that once echoed in a high school stadium now reverberated in massive arenas. Tim's journey from a quiet water boy to the best in the world became a tale etched in the annals of American football history.

"Gridiron Glory" wasn't just about touchdowns and victories; it was a testament to the transformative power of dedication, resilience, and the belief that anyone, regardless of their starting point, could achieve greatness on the hallowed turf of the gridiron.

Rhythm of the Ring

In the vibrant city of Harmonyville, a teenage boy named Malik discovered his rhythm in the unlikeliest of places—the boxing gym. Surrounded by the pulsating beats of determination, Malik's journey from the gritty streets to the grand stage of boxing unfolded like a symphony of triumph.

Malik's early years were steeped in challenges, but within him thrived a spirit that refused to be defeated. The boxing gym, a haven in the heart of adversity, became his refuge. The rhythmic dance of punches and the thud of gloves against the bag composed the soundtrack of Malik's resilience.

Coach Davis, a seasoned mentor with a keen eye, recognized Malik's potential. Under the dim lights of the gym, Malik's nimble footwork and lightning-fast jabs became a testament to his innate talent. The boxing ring, initially an intimidating battleground, transformed into Malik's canvas—a place where he painted his dreams with every disciplined step.

As Malik's prowess grew, so did his reputation. His fights weren't just displays of skill; they were performances that echoed the struggles of a young boy determined to carve his place in a world that often underestimated him. Malik's story spread beyond Harmonyville, reaching the ears of boxing legends and promoters.

Harmonyville's gritty streets witnessed the emergence of a future champion. Malik's journey became a beacon for aspiring boxers, especially young black talents who saw in him a reflection of their own dreams. The boxing gloves Malik wore weren't just a means of defense; they were symbols of resilience, breaking barriers with every powerful swing.

The grand arenas of professional boxing welcomed Malik with open arms. His fights were more than sporting events; they were celebrations of diversity, determination, and the unyielding spirit of a young black boxer who conquered the odds. Malik's journey, titled "Rhythm of the Ring," became an anthem of inspiration for generations to come.

Courage in Every Serve

In a small town nestled between rolling hills, lived a determined teenage girl named Maya. Despite the hardships that surrounded her, Maya found solace on the weathered tennis courts near her home. Her story was one of resilience, a testament to the fact that dreams could sprout even in the most unlikely of soils.

Maya's family struggled to make ends meet, but her love for tennis was boundless. The cracked courts, where weeds fought through the surface, became the proving grounds for Maya's unwavering spirit. With a worn-out racquet and shoes that had seen better days, she took her first steps toward a destiny that transcended her humble beginnings.

Coach Anderson, a retired tennis pro who saw potential in every determined player, recognized Maya's raw talent. With his guidance, Maya's game transformed. The rhythmic bounce of the ball and the swift movements of her feet became her daily anthem. Maya's forehand, a stroke of precision, echoed the resilience that defined her journey.

Word of Maya's prowess spread like wildfire. Tournaments that seemed worlds away became her battlegrounds. Her opponents, often hailing from privileged backgrounds, underestimated the girl with the worn racquet and the fire in her eyes. Maya's victories were not just on the scoreboard; they were triumphs over circumstances that sought to define her.

As Maya climbed the ranks, her story resonated beyond the tennis courts. A symbol of tenacity, she inspired a generation of aspiring athletes. Maya's journey from the dusty courts to the grand arenas was a beacon for those who dared to dream, proving that greatness could emerge from the most unexpected places.

The world watched in awe as Maya, the girl who once played on forgotten courts, stood tall on the grandest stage of tennis. Her story, titled "Courage in Every Serve," echoed in the hearts of young athletes, reminding them that dreams were not bound by circumstances but fueled by the courage to chase them.

Frozen Dreams

In the heart of a snow-kissed town, young Alex
faced a chilling reality when his father, a local hero
and renowned ice hockey player, passed away
unexpectedly. The echoes of the roaring crowd that
once cheered for his father were replaced by a
haunting silence. The ice rink, where dreams once
soared, became a melancholic reminder of what
was lost.

Alex, however, carried the legacy of his father on
slender shoulders. Despite the grief that shadowed
his every step, there was a fire within him ignited
by the memories of his father's triumphant goals
and the thunderous applause that followed. The ice
rink, once a place of sorrow, transformed into a
sanctuary where Alex sought solace and
inspiration.

With borrowed skates and a second-hand stick,
Alex took his first tentative steps onto the ice. The
cold wind bit at his face, but determination warmed
his heart. Guided by the spirit of his father, Alex's
skates sliced through the ice with a newfound
purpose. Every shot echoed the dreams of a father
and the aspirations of a son.

Coach Miller, an old friend of Alex's father, saw
the spark in the young boy's eyes. Under his
mentorship, Alex evolved from a grieving son to an

aspiring ice hockey prodigy. Late nights on the rink, practicing shots until the stars painted the sky, became Alex's routine. His resilience mirrored the icy surface he glided upon, unyielding and resilient.

As news of Alex's prowess spread, the town rekindled its love for ice hockey. The rink, once shrouded in sorrow, buzzed with excitement. Alex's journey to greatness wasn't just a personal triumph; it was a rallying point for a community that believed in the power of dreams.

The thunderous applause returned, this time not just for his father's memory but for the indomitable spirit of a teenage boy who turned grief into glory. Alex, now known as the "Frozen Dreamer," stood atop the ice hockey world, a testament to the transformative power of chasing one's dreams against all odds.

In the quiet town of Velocity Springs, where the hum of engines played a lullaby to its residents, lived a teenage boy named Jake. His world revolved around the local speedway, where dreams were born in the scent of burning rubber and the roar of powerful engines.

One fateful day, tragedy struck when Jake's father, a revered racer himself, met with a devastating car accident. The echoes of screeching tires and the ominous silence that followed left Jake's heart shattered. It was in that moment of loss that Jake found a burning desire to carry on his father's legacy, to race not only for victory but for the memory of the man who inspired him.

Guided by his father's spirit, Jake sought the mentorship of Old Man Thompson, a retired racer with tales of glory and scars to prove it. Under Thompson's watchful eye, Jake's hands, once trembling with grief, now gripped the steering wheel with newfound determination.

The local tracks became Jake's training ground, where he learned to navigate not only the asphalt but also the winding roads of grief. Each turn, each straightaway, became a metaphor for life's unpredictable journey.

As Jake progressed, he encountered challenges that mirrored the unpredictability of a race. From mechanical failures to fierce competitors, every obstacle was a test of his resilience. The scars on his car bore witness to the battles fought, and each victory became a triumph over adversity.

The day arrived when Jake, now a seasoned racer, faced his biggest challenge on the national stage. The memories of that car accident fueled his drive, and the roar of his engine echoed a promise to himself and the town that had rallied behind him.

In a climactic race that mirrored the rollercoaster of emotions he'd experienced, Jake emerged victorious. The checkered flag waved not only for a race won but for a journey completed. The stardust in Jake's eyes mirrored the twinkle of his father's star above, a constellation of triumph over tragedy.

Velocity Springs, once a town in mourning, now celebrated Jake as a racing legend. The scars of that car accident were transformed into badges of honor, telling a story of a boy who turned tragedy into triumph, grief into glory, and paved a road of stardust for generations to come.

Whispers of the Green

In the serene town of Fairway Pines, where gentle breezes whispered through emerald leaves, lived a teenage boy named Ethan. Unlike his peers, Ethan's heart danced to the rhythm of swinging clubs and the distant applause of the golf course.

From a young age, Ethan displayed an innate talent for golf that left seasoned players in awe. His journey to greatness began on the modest fairways of Fairway Pines Golf Club, where the grass seemed to bow to his every stroke.

Ethan's inspiration was his grandfather, a weathered golfer with tales of legendary courses and victories. Under Grandpa's watchful eye, Ethan honed his skills, absorbing the wisdom that echoed through the generations like a well-played putt.

As Ethan's reputation spread, he faced the challenge of entering the prestigious world of the PGA Tour. The first tournament was a symphony of nerves and excitement, the lush greens stretching endlessly before him. With every swing, Ethan showcased a mastery that transcended his age.
However, success didn't come without its share of hazards. Bunkers of self-doubt and water hazards of pressure tested Ethan's resolve. Yet, with unwavering determination, he navigated the course

of challenges, turning each setback into a strategic lesson.

Ethan's journey to becoming one of the best in the PGA Tour was a testament to discipline and passion. His victories weren't merely recorded in scorecards but etched into the hearts of those who witnessed his rise. The town of Fairway Pines, once a backdrop, now proudly boasted itself as the home of a golf prodigy.

In the pinnacle tournament that would define his legacy, Ethan faced the legendary players he once admired from afar. The fairways whispered encouragement, and the trees stood as silent spectators to the unfolding drama.

As the final putt rolled into the hole, Ethan's name ascended to the pinnacle of golfing glory. The cheers that erupted were not just for a victory but for the boy who turned a quaint town into a beacon of inspiration for aspiring golfers.

Ethan's journey, marked by dedication and love for the game, left an indelible mark on Fairway Pines and the PGA Tour. The whispers of the green carried his story to every golf course, an echo of a teenage boy who dared to dream and conquered the world one swing at a time.

Pedals of Perseverance

In the quaint town of Gearsville, where the hum of
spinning wheels resonated with ambition, lived a
teenage girl named Lily. Her journey into the world
of cycling began with a rusty bike and a heart full
of dreams.

Lily's fascination with cycling blossomed during
her daily rides to school, where she pedaled
through winding paths like a free spirit. The wind
tousled her hair, and the rhythmic click-clack of
her pedals became a melody of determination.

Recognizing Lily's potential, the town's seasoned
cyclists became her mentors. With their guidance,
she transformed her humble bike into a sleek
racing machine. The town soon buzzed with
excitement as Lily geared up for her first cycling
competition.

The race day arrived, and Gearsville's streets
transformed into a vibrant course of twists and
turns. Lily's heart pounded with anticipation as she
gripped the handlebars, ready to chase her dreams.
The cheers of the crowd blended with the whirring
of wheels as she surged forward.

Lily's journey, however, wasn't a smooth ride. She
faced steep hills of challenges and hairpin turns of
setbacks. Each fall became a stepping stone,

teaching her resilience and the importance of getting back on her bike.

As competitions unfolded on grander stages, Lily's prowess on the pedals became a symbol of perseverance. Her story resonated beyond Gearsville, inspiring young cyclists worldwide to embrace their passion and overcome obstacles.

In the pinnacle race that would define her legacy, Lily found herself among the world's elite cyclists. The course tested her endurance, but she pedaled on, fueled by a determination that knew no bounds. Crossing the finish line, she realized that her journey wasn't just about winning races; it was about empowering others to chase their dreams.

Lily's accolades in the world of cycling elevated Gearsville to a hub of inspiration. Cyclists from far and wide visited the town, hoping to absorb the spirit of the girl who turned ordinary streets into a velodrome of dreams.

As the sun set on another victorious day, Lily stood atop the podium, a symbol of grit and determination. Her story echoed through the streets of Gearsville and beyond, carried by the wind that had once whispered secrets to a girl with dreams as big as the open road.

Spike of Triumph

In the coastal town of Harmony Bay, where the rhythmic waves mirrored the spirit of its people, lived a teenage girl named Ava. Tall and agile, Ava's love for volleyball soared higher than the seagulls that graced the sandy shores.

From an early age, Ava found solace in the thud of a volleyball meeting her palms. The sun-kissed beaches of Harmony Bay became her training ground, and the salty breeze whispered secrets of the game. Ava's dreams stretched beyond the horizon, and her determination became as unyielding as the tides.

With makeshift nets and a circle of friends who shared her passion, Ava honed her skills. Her powerful spikes echoed the thunderous waves, drawing the attention of the town's seasoned volleyball coach, Coach Rodriguez. Recognizing Ava's potential, he became her mentor, sculpting raw talent into refined excellence.

Harmony Bay's humble volleyball court transformed into an arena of dreams. Ava's journey from local matches to national championships was marked by victories and defeats, each game teaching her valuable lessons about teamwork and resilience.
As Ava rose through the ranks, the town rallied

behind her. The cheers of "Spike it, Ava!" echoed in every match. But success didn't come without challenges. Ava faced formidable opponents, towering blockers, and moments of self-doubt. Yet, with each setback, her determination to conquer the volleyball court only intensified.

In the pivotal championship game that would determine her place among the world's best, Ava stood at the precipice of her dreams. The stadium roared with anticipation as she prepared for a match-deciding serve. With a powerful swing, Ava sent the ball soaring over the net, securing victory and etching her name in the annals of volleyball history.

Ava's story reverberated far beyond Harmony Bay, inspiring young athletes to pursue their passion for volleyball. The once-sleepy town became a pilgrimage site for volleyball enthusiasts, drawn by the aura of the girl who turned a simple game into a symphony of triumph.

As the sun dipped below the horizon, Ava stood on the beach, gazing at the vast expanse of the ocean. Her journey had been a testament to the power of dreams and the indomitable spirit of a teenage girl who soared to unparalleled heights, leaving an everlasting legacy on the sands of Harmony Bay.

Rhythmic Rally

In the bustling city of Dynamo Heights, where the cityscape was a symphony of lights, lived a teenage girl named Zoe. Petite but full of energy, Zoe's heart danced to the rhythmic beats of table tennis. The local community center with its vibrant table tennis tables became her sanctuary.

From the click-clack of paddles to the crisp sound of a well-executed serve, Zoe's passion for table tennis was infectious. Her journey began with friendly matches against the neighborhood kids, but her talent soon outgrew the local scene. Coach Martinez, a seasoned table tennis maestro, spotted Zoe's potential and took her under his wing.

Under Coach Martinez's guidance, Zoe's skills evolved. Her swift movements and precision on the table earned her the nickname "Rhythmic Zoe." The local tournaments were stepping stones, and Zoe glided through them with an elegance that mirrored a well-choreographed dance.

As news of Zoe's prowess spread, invitations poured in for national competitions. Dynamo Heights cheered for their table tennis prodigy, and Zoe's matches became the highlight of every tournament. With each victory, she carried the dreams of her city on her shoulders.

The path to international acclaim was not without its challenges. Zoe faced opponents with diverse playing styles, each match a unique composition of strategies. But Zoe's resilience and love for the game became her guiding forces.

In the climactic world championship, Zoe found herself facing the reigning champion. The arena pulsated with excitement as Zoe engaged in a fierce rally. Her movements were a blend of skill and finesse, mesmerizing the spectators. In a nail-biting finish, Zoe secured the winning point, claiming the title of the world's best table tennis player.

Dynamo Heights erupted in joy, and Zoe became a hometown hero. The community center transformed into a shrine of inspiration, with young table tennis enthusiasts emulating Zoe's signature moves. She dedicated her victory to Coach Martinez and the city that nurtured her talent.

Zoe's journey from local matches to global triumphs echoed the sentiment that passion, coupled with dedication, could turn a simple game into a masterpiece. As the city lights glittered in celebration, Zoe stood proud, a rhythmic champion who had etched her name in the lively beats of Dynamo Heights.

Tall Warrior's Triumph

In the serene hills of Eastwood Village lived a lanky teenager named Jake, whose journey to becoming a Taekwondo maestro was nothing short of extraordinary. Towering over his peers, Jake's height became his strength, and his heart harbored the spirit of a warrior.

From a young age, Jake was drawn to the disciplined world of martial arts. The local dojo, nestled amid lush greenery, became his training ground. Sensei Kato, a wise and seasoned Taekwondo master, recognized Jake's potential early on and became his mentor.

Jake's training was rigorous, and his dedication was unwavering. The swaying trees and rustling leaves bore witness to his countless kicks and precise movements. Jake's legs, like tree trunks, moved with grace and power, earning him the nickname "Tall Warrior" among his peers.

As Jake progressed through the ranks, his reputation echoed through the martial arts community. The regional championships became his arena, where opponents marveled at the agility hidden within his towering frame. The applause of the spectators transformed into a rhythmic beat that fueled Jake's determination.

Word of Jake's prowess reached beyond borders, and soon he found himself representing Eastwood Village in the prestigious Asian Taekwondo Championship. The bustling city of Seoul hosted the event, and Jake, with his head held high, stepped onto the grand stage.

Facing opponents from diverse cultures, Jake's height became a symbol of his unique strength. His kicks soared like mountain peaks, and his blocks were as solid as ancient stones. With each match, Jake embodied the essence of Taekwondo, a harmonious blend of power, precision, and respect.

In the final showdown, Jake faced a formidable opponent from Japan. The air was charged with anticipation as the two warriors engaged in a spirited exchange of kicks and punches. In a breathtaking climax, Jake executed a flawless spinning kick, securing victory and the title of Asia's best Taekwondo practitioner.

Eastwood Village erupted in joy, and Jake returned home not just as a champion but as a symbol of perseverance and courage. The dojo, once a serene haven, transformed into a bustling hub as aspiring martial artists flocked to learn from the Tall Warrior.

Jake's journey proved that greatness knows no height, and a determined heart can overcome any challenge. As the sun set over Eastwood Village, Jake stood tall, not just in stature but as a beacon of inspiration for generations to come.

Riding Waves of Triumph

Meet Max, a lanky teenager with an insatiable passion for surfing that matched the vastness of Australia's coastal horizons. Towering over the golden beaches, Max's journey to becoming one of the country's best surfers was as exhilarating as the waves he conquered.

From the age of twelve, Max found solace in the rhythmic melody of crashing waves. The salty breeze and the endless expanse of the Pacific Ocean became his playground. The local surf club, nestled between sand dunes, witnessed Max's early attempts and echoed with the laughter of fellow surf enthusiasts.

Under the mentorship of an old, weathered surfer named Pete, Max's skills evolved. Pete, a sage of the ocean, taught him not just to ride the waves but to understand their language. Max's surfboard became an extension of his being, and the ocean, a trusted companion.

As the years passed, Max's reputation soared along with the waves he conquered. The shimmering beaches of Bondi and the roaring breaks of Bells Beach became his testing grounds. He participated in local competitions, where his tall frame glided effortlessly over the waves, earning him the nickname "Giant of the Surf."

Max's true challenge awaited at the Australian Junior Surfing Championship, where the country's finest young surfers converged. The azure waters of the Gold Coast set the stage for an epic showdown. With determination etched on his face, Max rode each wave with a blend of skill and grace that left spectators in awe.

In the championship's final heat, Max faced a formidable opponent, a surfer with a string of victories. The ocean seemed to hush in anticipation as the two surfers paddled into position. In a breathtaking climax, Max executed a flawless aerial maneuver, soaring above the cresting wave and clinching victory.

The news of Max's triumph echoed through coastal towns, and he became an inspiration for aspiring surfers nationwide. Max's story wasn't just about conquering waves; it was a testament to resilience, respect for nature, and the joy of pursuing one's passion.

As the sun dipped below the horizon, Max stood tall against the backdrop of the shimmering sea, his surfboard raised in triumph. The waves whispered their approval, and Max, the tall boy with a heart as vast as the ocean, became a legend among the rolling tides of Australia's surf culture.

Snowbound Dreams

Meet Jake, a towering teenager whose heart soared with the crisp mountain air and the thrill of conquering snow-covered peaks. Nestled in the embrace of the Alps, Jake's journey to becoming one of the world's best snowboarders was as exhilarating as the descents he carved into the powder.

From the age of thirteen, Jake found his calling on the snow-laden slopes. His towering frame, seemingly defying gravity, became a familiar sight against the backdrop of pristine white landscapes. The local snowboarding community, a tight-knit group of enthusiasts, witnessed Jake's early attempts and cheered on his every descent.

Under the guidance of his mentor, a seasoned snowboarder named Elena, Jake's skills evolved. Elena, with her wild mane of silver hair, taught him not just to navigate the slopes but to dance with the snow. Jake's snowboard became an extension of his identity, and the mountains, his grand stage.

As the years passed, Jake's reputation echoed through the alpine valleys and across international snowboarding circuits. Competing in events like the Winter X Games, he defied gravity with jaw-dropping tricks and embraced the icy challenges that awaited him.

The pinnacle of Jake's snowboarding odyssey arrived at the Winter Olympics, where the world's finest snowboarders converged. The powdery slopes of the Swiss Alps set the stage for a breathtaking showdown. With adrenaline coursing through his veins, Jake descended the mountain with a blend of precision and flair that left spectators in awe.

In the Olympic final, Jake faced a formidable opponent, a seasoned competitor with a string of accolades. The snow-laden arena fell silent as the two snowboarders prepared for their descent. In a spectacular climax, Jake executed a gravity-defying jump, twisting and turning mid-air, securing victory and etching his name in snowboarding history.

News of Jake's triumph cascaded through snowy landscapes, and he became an inspiration for aspiring snowboarders worldwide. Jake's story wasn't just about conquering slopes; it was a testament to courage, camaraderie, and the joy of chasing one's dreams.

As the sun dipped behind snow-capped peaks, Jake stood tall against the canvas of the Alps, his snowboard raised in triumph. The mountains

echoed with the cheers of fellow snowboarders,
and Jake, the tall boy with a spirit as boundless as
the snow, became a legend among the peaks and
valleys of the snowboarding world.

Strength Beyond Measure

In a small town where laughter and joy filled the air, there lived a teenager named Max, whose infectious smile belied the challenges he faced. Max, a cheerful and resilient boy, found solace in the warmth of his family and the iron weights that awaited him in the garage.

Max's school days were a test of his spirit. Teased and taunted for his weight, he carried the burden of judgment on shoulders that would one day become pillars of strength. Instead of succumbing to the weight of negativity, Max turned to weightlifting as a refuge, an outlet for his emotions and a path to self-discovery.

Guided by his uncle, a former weightlifting champion, Max learned the art and science of lifting. The garage transformed into Max's sanctuary, where the clinking of weights echoed his determination. With each lift, he shed not just the physical weight but also the emotional baggage that held him back.

Max's journey into weightlifting wasn't just about building muscles; it was a transformative experience that sculpted his character. His daily regimen became a testament to discipline and perseverance. As the weights increased, so did Max's resolve to prove that strength comes in all shapes and sizes.

News of Max's dedication reached the ears of a renowned weightlifting coach, and soon, Max found himself training with the best. The gym, once a haven of solitude, became a vibrant arena where Max honed his skills alongside seasoned athletes. His camaraderie with fellow weightlifters transcended judgments, fostering an environment of acceptance and encouragement.

The pinnacle of Max's journey unfolded at the World Weightlifting Championship. Against formidable opponents, Max stood on the grand stage, his once-teased physique now a symbol of resilience. The barbell, laden with dreams and determination, soared into the air as Max lifted not just the weights but the hopes of everyone who had faced adversity.

Max's triumph rippled beyond the weightlifting community. His story became an inspiration for those who felt weighed down by societal expectations. Max, the once-teased boy, stood atop the podium, a beacon of strength and self-acceptance.

Back in his small town, Max's schoolmates, once purveyors of ridicule, now cheered for the hometown hero. Max had not just lifted weights; he had lifted the collective spirit of a community. The echoes of applause, once distant, now resonated in the heart of a boy who turned adversity into triumph, proving that true strength indeed lies beyond measure.

Aim for the Stars

In a quaint village nestled between rolling hills and azure skies, lived a teenager named Olivia with a passion that soared higher than the birds that danced in the open skies. Olivia's heart belonged to the world of precision and focus—she was destined to be a rifle shooter.

From a young age, Olivia found solace in the rhythmic heartbeat of her rifle. The stock nestled into her shoulder felt like an extension of her being, and the target downrange became a canvas for her dreams. The quietude of the shooting range was her sanctuary, where concentration painted her path to greatness.

Olivia's journey began in the backyard, where makeshift targets were pinned to the fence. Her father, a veteran shooter, recognized the spark in her eyes and became her first mentor. With each shot, Olivia's aim grew truer, and her resolve deepened.

As the sun dipped below the horizon, Olivia's backyard escapades evolved into serious training. The local shooting range became her second home, and the pop of gunfire echoed her aspirations. Driven by dreams of Olympic glory, Olivia embraced a rigorous training regimen, mastering the delicate dance between breath and trigger.

The journey to the Olympics was not without hurdles. Olivia faced skeptics who believed shooting was a sport best left to others. Yet, undeterred, she shouldered her rifle and aimed for the stars. Her dedication drew the attention of a seasoned coach who saw in her the potential to leave an indelible mark on the world stage.

The Olympic arena, with its towering expectations, became the canvas where Olivia painted her masterpiece. Each shot told a story of resilience, focus, and unwavering determination. The spectators, once unfamiliar faces, now roared in applause as Olivia's bullets found their mark with unerring precision.

The medal draped around Olivia's neck wasn't just a symbol of victory; it was a testament to a journey marked by countless hours of practice, unwavering belief, and a spirit that refused to be confined. Back in her village, the cheers echoed through the hills, and Olivia became a beacon of inspiration for aspiring shooters.

As the sun set on the Olympic stage, Olivia's heart swelled with gratitude. She had not just won a medal; she had carved her name into the annals of history. The girl from the quaint village had become one of the best rifle shooters in the world, proving that dreams, when nurtured with passion and persistence, can propel you to heights beyond imagination.

Archer's Symphony

In a charming town embraced by lush forests and babbling brooks, lived a teenage girl named Elizabeth, whose heart sang to the tune of twanging bowstrings and soaring arrows. Elizabeth was destined to be an archer, and her journey to greatness was destined to become a melody in the symphony of sports.

From the moment she laid eyes on a bow, Elizabeth felt a connection as if the ancient weapon whispered secrets only she could comprehend. The archery range, with its neatly aligned targets, became her canvas, and every arrow she loosed was a stroke in her masterpiece.

Elizabeth's journey began with a weathered bow handed down by her grandfather, a seasoned archer in his youth. Under the sprawling oak trees in her backyard, Elizabeth learned the art of archery. The wind whispered guidance, and the rustling leaves became her audience.

As Elizabeth's skill burgeoned, so did her dreams. The local archery club became her second home, where camaraderie blossomed, and mentors recognized her innate talent. With a quiver full of determination, Elizabeth set her sights on the grandest stage—the Olympics.

The path to Olympic glory was no cakewalk. Elizabeth faced challenges that tested her resilience and aimed to sway her from her chosen trajectory. Critics questioned her choice, but Elizabeth, with unwavering resolve, silenced them with arrows that found their mark with unparalleled precision.

Training became a ritual, and Elizabeth's bow became an extension of her arm. The rhythmic pull of the string echoed her determination, and every bullseye was a testament to her dedication. Coaches marveled at her technique, and fellow athletes admired the grace with which she approached her craft.

When Elizabeth stepped onto the Olympic archery range, it was not just as a competitor but as a maestro ready to conduct a symphony of skill and precision. The tension in the air mirrored the drawn bowstring, and as Elizabeth's arrows sailed through the air, they seemed to dance to a tune only she could hear.

The gold medal draped around Elizabeth's neck was not just a reward; it was the crescendo of years of practice, belief, and an unyielding spirit. The town that once echoed with the rustling of leaves now resounded with cheers, as Elizabeth had become one of the best archers in the world, proving that dreams, like arrows, can find their mark when released with passion and purpose.

In the coastal town of Harbor Haven, where the sun painted the sea with hues of gold, lived a teenager named Matt. Born with a spirit as boundless as the ocean, Matt faced life with an unyielding determination, overcoming the challenges of a physical disability. Little did he know that his indomitable spirit would carry him to the pinnacle of success in the world of para swimming.

Matt's aquatic journey began in the community pool, a haven where the water became a source of liberation. The rhythmic movements of his arms, guided by an unwavering will, created ripples that echoed resilience. The local swim coach recognized not just his strokes but the courage that surged with every lap.

As Matt's skill blossomed, so did his aspirations. He transitioned from the community pool to the vastness of the ocean, where his dreams expanded like the horizon. The water, once seen as a challenge, became a realm of infinite possibilities.

Competing in regional para championships, Matt's prowess became a beacon of inspiration. His body, in graceful defiance of expectations, moved through the water with a strength that defied limitations. The journey to the Paralympics became a testament to breaking barriers and rewriting

narratives.
Training sessions at dawn and twilight became rituals of empowerment. Coaches marveled not just at his physical prowess but the resilience that flowed through his veins. Fellow para-athletes found in Matt a symbol of triumph over adversity.

When the grand day arrived at the Paralympic pool, Matt stood at the edge, his heart synchronized with the rhythmic beat of anticipation. The whistle blew, and like a force of nature, Matt surged forward. The water responded to his tenacity, propelling him to unprecedented speeds.

As Matt touched the wall, claiming victory, the cheers echoed louder than the waves. The gold medal draped around his neck wasn't just a symbol of triumph; it was a testament to a journey fueled by unyielding spirit, perseverance, and the belief that one can navigate any depth with resilience.

Harbor Haven, once a quiet town, now resonated with the applause of triumph. Matt, the para-swimmer, had not just conquered the waters; he had conquered preconceptions. His story, like the ripples he created, spread far and wide, inspiring generations to dive into their dreams, for in the sea of challenges, one could discover the strength to swim against any tide.

In the heart of Tokyo, amidst the echoes of tradition and the pulse of modernity, lived a teenage boy named Hiroshi. His journey, unlike any other, unfolded in the disciplined arena of judo, where he emerged not only as a skilled martial artist but as the beacon of a new era.

From a young age, Hiroshi was drawn to the philosophy of judo, where strength wasn't just physical but a harmonious blend of mind, body, and spirit. His days began with the rising sun, casting its golden glow on the dojo where he honed his skills. Sensei Takashi, the venerable judo master, recognized Hiroshi's potential, not just in technique but in the unwavering spirit he brought to the mat.

Hiroshi's journey transcended the boundaries of the dojo; it became a cultural odyssey. He immersed himself in the teachings of ancient samurais, understanding that true strength lay in respect, humility, and the ability to uplift others. His journey became a fusion of tradition and innovation, a testament to the resilience of a rising sun warrior.

Regional championships bore witness to Hiroshi's prowess. His opponents marveled not just at the precision of his throws but the tranquility that emanated from within. Hiroshi, like the sakura blossoms in spring, showcased the beauty of balance and control.

As he progressed to the Asian Judo Championships, Hiroshi faced opponents from diverse cultures. Each match became a cultural exchange, a celebration of diversity through the universal language of judo. The arena, electrified with the spirit of competition, also echoed with mutual respect and camaraderie.

The pinnacle awaited Hiroshi at the Asian Games, where the world watched in awe as he faced the best in the continent. His every move was a dance, a choreography of discipline and grace. When the final bow was taken, Hiroshi stood victorious, not just as a judo champion but as a symbol of unity in diversity.

Hiroshi's story didn't end with medals and accolades; it resonated in the hearts of aspiring judokas across Asia. He became a mentor, teaching not just techniques but the essence of judo—a way of life. Hiroshi's legacy wasn't just about winning on the mat; it was about winning the hearts of those who believed in the boundless potential within.

In the dojo of life, Hiroshi's journey continues, for

the rising sun warrior knows that the path to greatness is paved not just with victories but with the indomitable spirit that rises with every challenge, casting a light that inspires generations to come.

Eclatant Acrobat

In the picturesque town of Marseille, a teenage dreamer named Julien leaped into the world of gymnastics, painting the skies with his agile moves and illuminating the hearts of all who witnessed his brilliance.

Julien's journey began in a quaint gymnasium where chalk dust danced in the air, and the rhythmic claps echoed the rhythm of determination. From somersaults to splits, Julien embraced the challenges with the grace of a French sonnet, transforming the mat into his poetic canvas.

His coach, Madame Lacroix, recognized not just Julien's physical prowess but the artistic flair he brought to gymnastics. The parallel bars became his lyrical notes, the vault his grand crescendo. Every routine was a performance, a symphony of strength and elegance that set him apart on the European gymnastics stage.

As the sun dipped behind the Eiffel Tower, Julien soared to new heights at the European Gymnastics Championships. The arenas echoed with "Allez Julien!" as he executed flawless routines, earning him not only medals but the adoration of fans across the continent.

Julien's journey wasn't just about medals; it was a

celebration of artistic expression. His floor routines were like ballet, each movement telling a story of resilience and passion. The balance beam, a narrow path of challenges, showcased Julien's unwavering focus and precision.

The European Games became Julien's pièce de résistance. The crowd gasped at his daring feats, and judges were enchanted by the poetry in his movements. When the tricolor flag was raised, Julien stood on the podium, not just as a gymnastics champion but as a symbol of artistic triumph.

Beyond the medals, Julien's story unfolded as an inspiration to young gymnasts across Europe. He became a mentor, teaching that gymnastics wasn't just about physical strength but about expressing oneself through the language of the body. His gymnasium transformed into a haven where dreams took flight.

Julien's legacy wasn't confined to the gym; it resonated in the cobbled streets of Marseille. The local children, inspired by his journey, somersaulted in playgrounds, dreaming of becoming the next "Eclatant Acrobat."

In the twilight of his competitive career, Julien

knew that his true victory was in the hearts he touched. As he gracefully bowed out, he left behind a legacy that continued to shine, proving that the spirit of a gymnast wasn't measured by the height of their jumps but by the impact of their dreams.

The Chess Maestro

In the labyrinthine streets of Moscow, where history whispered through the air, a young prodigy named Nikolai discovered his passion for chess. It all began in a quaint bookstore, where an old chess set beckoned to him. Little did he know, those dusty chess pieces would set the stage for a symphony of intellect and resilience.

Nikolai's mentor, the enigmatic Grandmaster Ivanov, recognized a spark within him. Under Ivanov's tutelage, Nikolai's chess prowess blossomed. The chessboard, a realm of endless possibilities, transformed into Nikolai's sanctuary—a place where the clatter of pieces echoed the cadence of his burgeoning genius.

As Nikolai delved deeper into the world of chess, the city itself became a character in his story. The Red Square, the Kremlin, and the spires of St. Basil's Cathedral witnessed the young maestro honing his craft. Each move became a strategic dance, a silent conversation between two minds engaged in the battle of wits.

Local tournaments became Nikolai's proving ground. The "Pawn's Waltz," as it came to be known, was a spectacle that drew spectators from all corners of Moscow. Nikolai, with an air of quiet confidence, navigated the chessboard like a maestro conducting an orchestra, leaving opponents in awe.

Grandmaster Ivanov guided Nikolai to national championships, where his reputation as a chess prodigy took flight. His story became a legend in the making, whispered across the chess community like a secret passage to greatness.

The pinnacle of Nikolai's journey awaited him on the grand stage of the World Chess Championship. The world watched in anticipation as he faced off against international titans. The chess pieces seemed to come alive under his command, performing a ballet of strategy that left spectators breathless.

But "The Chess Maestro" was more than a tale of victories. It was a narrative of growth, friendship, and the power of mentorship. Nikolai's bond with Grandmaster Ivanov transcended chess; it became a beacon of guidance and wisdom that illuminated Nikolai's path.

In the quiet moments between moves, Nikolai reflected on the lessons chess had taught him—patience in planning, resilience in defeat, and the art of turning setbacks into comebacks. His journey, symbolized by the triumphant checkmate on the grandest stage, was a testament to the enduring power of intellect and the boundless potential within every young mind.

"The Chess Maestro" echoed through the hallowed halls of chess lore, inspiring generations to come. Nikolai's legacy wasn't just etched on a chessboard; it was woven into the very fabric of Moscow's chess history, forever remembered as the prodigy who turned every move into a masterpiece.